BLOOMSBURY CHILDREN'S BOOKS
Bloomsbury Publishing Plc
50 Bedford Square, London, WC1B 3DP, UK

BLOOMSBURY, BLOOMSBURY CHILDREN'S BOOKS
and the Diana logo are trademarks of Bloomsbury Publishing Plc

First published in Great Britain 2019 by Bloomsbury Publishing Plc

A catalogue record for this book is available from the British Library

ISBN: HB: 978 1 4088 8560 4; PB: 978 1 4088 8561 1; eBook: 978 1 4088 8562 8

2 4 6 8 10 9 7 5 3 1

Printed in China by Leo Paper Products, Heshan, Guangdong
All papers used by Bloomsbury Publishing Plc are natural, recyclable products from
wood grown in well managed forests. The manufacturing processes conform to
the environmental regulations of the country of origin

To find out more about our authors and books visit
www.bloomsbury.com and sign up for our newsletters

For Mya, with Little
Monster love ~ S.P-H.

To Jason ~ A.R.

Smriti Prasadam-Halls   Angie Rozelaar

Don't Make Me CROSS!

BLOOMSBURY
CHILDREN'S BOOKS
LONDON   OXFORD   NEW YORK   NEW DELHI   SYDNEY

I'm a little monster!
I am smiley, small and sweet,
with gorgeous little monster eyes
and furry monster feet.

There's just one thing
that you should know . . .

I HAVE TO BE THE BOSS.

And if you don't remember . . .

... I'll get very, **VERY CROSS!**

Here's my happy monster face –
today's my birthday tea!
All my friends are coming round
to celebrate with me.

I'm welcoming my buddies in
and everything is fine,
but . . .

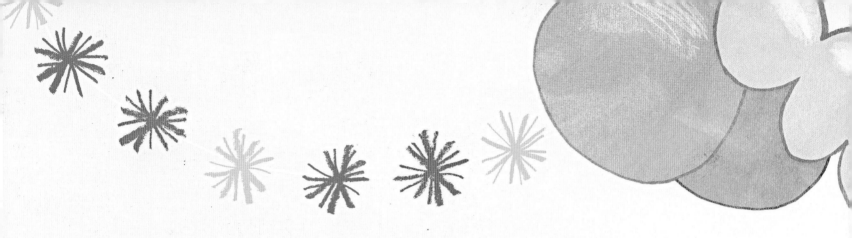

Don't forget these presents . . .

. . . are ALL MINE!

On the Monster Bouncy Castle
I can do BIG jumps!

BOUNCY-BOUNCY up and down . . .

. . . and then it's Monster Bumps!

And next comes Monster Statues –
are you ready to begin?
This game is really excellent . . .

BUT ONLY IF I WIN!

My birthday tea is ready - SLUUUURP! Delicious monster treats,

like slimy chocolate mouse balls and hairy spider sweets.

I DO NOT like this party, STOMP!
It isn't any fun.

We're playing monster hide and seek —
but WHERE IS everyone?

I stomp my monster feet and yell out . . .

RAAH!

RAAH!

RAAH!

You'd better all come out RIGHT NOW,
WHEREVER YOU . . .

AAAAAAAR

YUCK!

There's **jelly** sliding down my NOSE

and **bug eyes** on my FACE!

There's **wiggly worms**

between my TOES...

and EVERY other place!

I'm SITTING in the **spiders**

and there's **custard** down my TUMMY.

There's **ice cream** on my BOTTOM

and my FUR is stuck with **honey!**

Oh dear . . .
I've been a silly monster,
I can see I wasn't fair.

I'm sorry, everybody . . .
Let me show you **I** can SHARE.

I'm a little monster,
I am smiley, small and sweet,
with gorgeous little monster eyes
and furry monster feet.

And **I NEVER** will be grumpy now,
I NEVER will be cross . . .

As long as every now and then,

I GET TO BE THE BOSS!